CHRISTMAS POST OFFICE

WITH BEST CHRISTMAS WISHES

D0364247

For Miss Eloise Jingle,
Holly Berry House,
Plum Pudding Lane,
Great Christmasingham

For my lovely, generous and utterly bonkers grandmas,

Alice and Betty

x

First published 2020 by Macmillan Children's Books
an imprint of Pan Macmillan
The Smithson, 6 Briset Street, London, EC1M 5NR
Associated companies throughout the world
www.panmacmillan.com

ISBN 978-1-5290-4337-2

3 5 7 9 8 6 4 2

A CIP catalogue record for this book is available from the British Library.

Design by Alison Still

Printed and bound in Poland

Alex T. Smith

The Twelve Days of Christmas

or

Grandma is Overly Generous

MACMILLAN CHILDREN'S BOOKS

On the first day of Christmas
my grandma gave to me . . .

a partridge in a pear tree.

WITH
BEST CHRISTMAS WISHES

WITH
BEST CHRISTMAS WISHES

Ms TRUDY TRUELOVE'S

LOVEBIRDS OF DISTINCTION

On the second day of Christmas
my grandma gave to me . . .

two turtle doves
and a partridge in a pear tree.

On the third day of Christmas
my grandma gave to me . . .

three french hens,
two turtle doves
and a partridge in a pear tree.

GERALD McSQUAWK'S
FEATHERED FRIENDS
RESCUE CENTRE

DIRECT FROM THE TROPICS

On the fourth day of Christmas
my grandma gave to me . . .

four calling birds,
three french hens,
two turtle doves
and a partridge in a pear tree.

On the fifth day of Christmas
my grandma gave to me . . .

five gold rings.

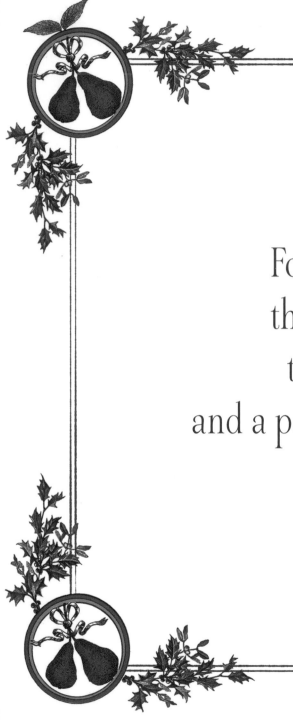

Four calling birds,
three french hens,
two turtle doves
and a partridge in a pear tree.

CHOCOLATIERS

Mme. DANDINEMENT & DAUGHTERS

SUISSE

EXPRESS DELIVERY

On the sixth day of Christmas
my grandma gave to me . . .

six geese a-laying.

Five gold rings,
four calling birds,
three french hens,
two turtle doves
and a partridge in a pear tree.

THE RUB-A-DUB HOME PAMPER SERVICE

On the seventh day of Christmas
my grandma gave to me . . .

seven squirrels

a-snorkelling.

Six geese a-laying,
five gold rings,
four calling birds,
three french hens,
two turtle doves
and a partridge in a pear tree.

On the eighth day of Christmas
my grandma gave to me . . .

eight bears

a-balancing.

Seven squirrels a-snorkelling,
six geese a-laying,
five gold rings,
four calling birds,
three french hens,
two turtle doves
and a partridge in a pear tree.

MERRY CHRISTMAS
FROM THE POST OFFICE

HOGG & BONGO LTD
PERCUSSION PROVIDERS

LITTLE DRUMMER BOY • HOME DELIVERY SERVICE •

On the ninth day of Christmas
my grandma gave to me . . .

nine drummers

drumming.

Eight bears a-balancing,
seven squirrels a-snorkelling,
six geese a-laying,
five gold rings,
four calling birds,
three french hens,
two turtle doves
and a partridge in a pear tree.

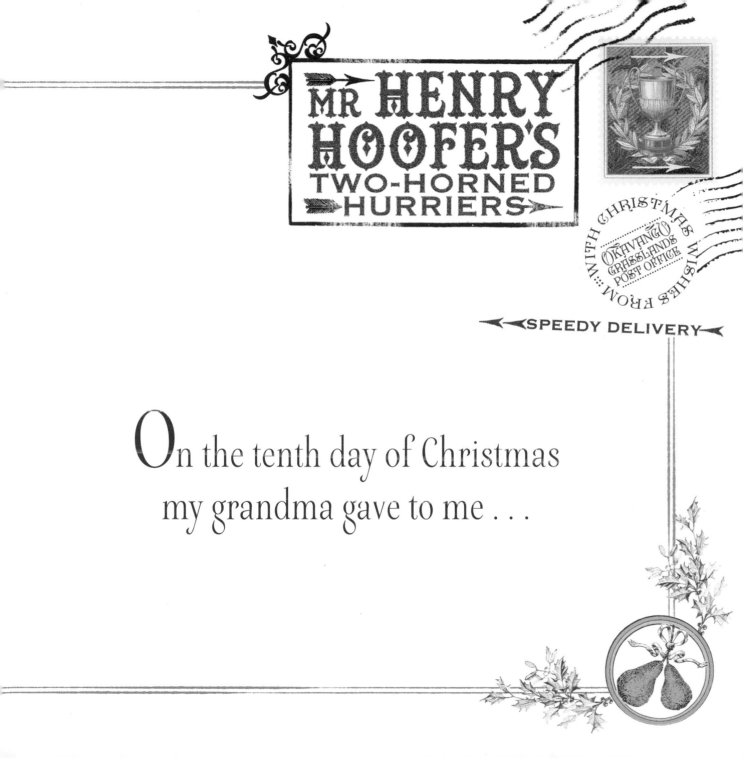

MR **HENRY HOOFER'S** TWO-HORNED HURRIERS

◄◄ **SPEEDY DELIVERY** ◄

On the tenth day of Christmas
my grandma gave to me . . .

ten rhinos racing.

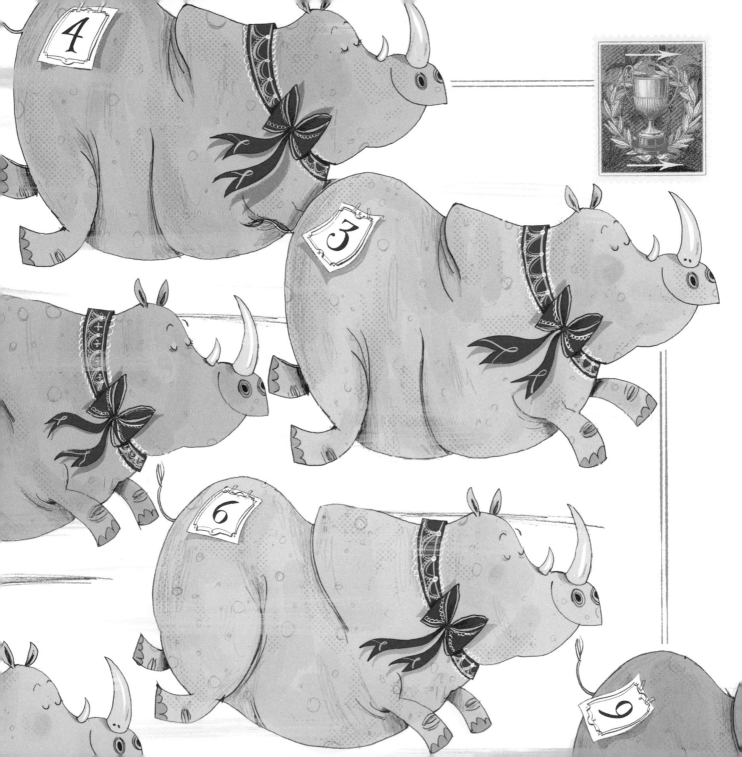

Nine drummers drumming,
eight bears a-balancing,
seven squirrels a-snorkelling,
six geese a-laying,
five gold rings,
four calling birds,
three french hens,
two turtle doves
and a partridge in a pear tree.

ANTARCTIC GENERAL POST·OFFICE

SOUTH POLE EXPRESS
PARCEL DELIVERY

THE
ROYAL
TUNDRA
TOWN BAND
EST. 1867

On the eleventh day of Christmas
my grandma gave to me . . .

eleven penguins parping.

Ten rhinos racing,
nine drummers drumming,
eight bears a-balancing,
seven squirrels a-snorkelling,
six geese a-laying,
five gold rings,
four calling birds,
three french hens,
two turtle doves
and a partridge in a pear tree.

FRAGILE

EXPRESS DELIVERY

HANDLE
WITH
GREAT
CARE

THIS WAY
UP

IF IT IS

EXTRA LARGE

THE
EXTRA LARGE
PARCEL COMPANY

WE ARE

IN CHARGE

On the twelfth day of Christmas
my grandma gave to me . . .

SOCKS.

Eleven penguins parping,
ten rhinos racing,
nine drummers drumming,
eight bears a-balancing,
seven squirrels a-snorkelling,
six geese a-laying,

five gold rings,
four calling birds,
three french hens,
two turtle doves
and a partridge in a pear tree.

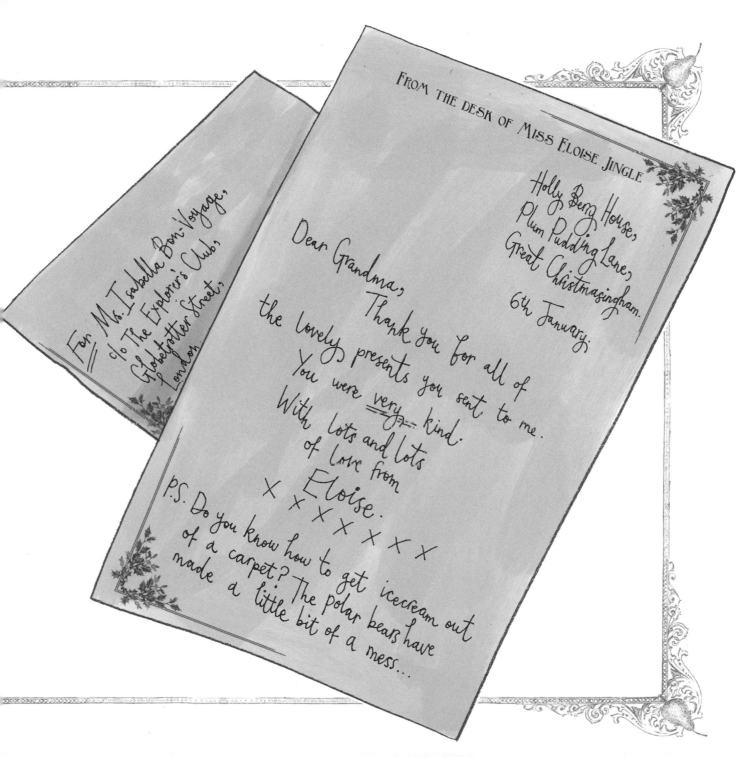

FROM THE DESK OF MISS ELOISE JINGLE

Holly Berry House,
Plum Pudding Lane,
Great Christmasingham.

6th January.

Dear Grandma,
        Thank you for all of
the lovely presents you sent to me.
        You were very kind.
        With lots and lots
                of love from
                Eloise.
        X X X X X X

P.S. Do you know how to get icecream out
    of a carpet? The polar bears have
    made a little bit of a mess...

For Ms. Isabella Bon-Voyage,
c/o The Explorer's Club,
Globetrotter Street,
London.

A Note from Alex T. Smith

The idea for this version of *The Twelve Days of Christmas* came to me when I found myself humming the tune and then struggling to remember what was gifted on which day. In the end I started to make it up and the result is this book.

It was interesting then when researching the original lyrics (after being unable to remember what they were) that the poem has been around in some form for centuries, and it is believed to have begun as a cumulative memory game. (A game I'd have failed!)

It wasn't until 1909 that the English composer Frederic Austin set the verses to music that it became the carol we all know (or think we know!) today. Discovering this last fact informed my illustrations as I decided to set this book in the late Edwardian period in homage to the creation of the carol. Researching Edwardian packaging and postage has been a real treat, as has creating Eloise's extensive wardrobe. Many of her outfits are based on real clothing from the time (so many frills!) although I may have taken a few liberties with colours and patterns. I have, in some place, also just made up my own designs entirely.

This book has also allowed me to indulge in my love of sending things in the post. Although it has left me wondering quite how Eloise's grandmother managed to send some of the items through the mail . . .

But that's grandmas for you – wonderful, but utterly bonkers.